NOT
Just Another
Self-Defence Book

A Streetproofing for Kids Series

Volume 1

by
Hugh B. Wilson
& John W. Yee

Outgoing Press
Toronto

Printed in Canada by University of Toronto Press Inc.
5201 Dufferin Street
North York, Ontario, Canada
M3H 5T8

ISBN 1-896212-01-8

Outgoing Press
P.O. Box 45507
747 Don Mills road
Don Mills, Ontario
M3C 3S4

Canadian Cataloguing in Publication Data

Wilson, Hugh Barrington
    Not Just Another Self-Defence Book

(A streetproofing for kids series; v. 1)
ISBN 1-896212-01-8

1. Self-defence - Juvenile literature. 2. Martial arts - Juvenile literature.
Yee, John William. II. Title. III. Series.

GV1111.W55 1996   j796.8   C94-932349-7

She took my hand and squeezed it. "You sold yourself short. You could've been more than a teacher and a coach."

I returned the squeeze and said, "Listen to me, Savannah. There's no word in the language I revere more than *teacher*. None. My heart sings when someone refers to me as his or her teacher and it always has. I've honored myself and the entire family of man by becoming one."

The Prince of Tides, by Pat Conroy

DISCLAIMER

This book is for information purposes only. The authors, editors, publisher, or distributors of this book disclaim any liability from any damage or injuries of any type that a reader may encounter from the use of said information.

CONTENTS

To Mom and Dad

INTRODUCTION

Dear Parents:

"Why is this called 'Not Just Another Self-Defence Book'?" you might ask.

There are several reasons why we thought that the title is appropriate:

1. First, two authors have wrote it. It is very unusual for two people to write about martial arts because there is a lot of controversy as to what is correct and what is not; but the old saying "two heads are better than one" still applies despite the difficult subject matter. The end result is a book that excels anything that we could have written individually.

2. Next, we specialize in teaching kids. The information is designed especially for them. Although it is suitable for adults as well, it may not be appropriate if it was the other way around: that is, if you gave a martial arts book that was intended for adults to kids. Some of the techniques which may work wonders for grown-ups might be disastrous for juveniles; in any given confrontation, your child is most likely to be up against someone who is taller, heavier, and stronger.

3. To compensate for that, kids must have other tools that will give them more of an advantage. For example, if they were not told that running is an important option in self-defence, then they might think that they must always stand their ground and fight to the bitter end no matter what. (Refer to what we really mean by self-defence in the section on "What is Self-Defence".)

Confronting someone directly is often the answer for some people like a 350 pounds bouncer who has experience in that sort of thing, but it is not the best option for kids.

4. That is why we have included several streetproofing topics like Trust, Avoidance, Awareness, and Safety. Even the youngest students at this level will have an edge over someone who is bigger and stronger once they realize that it is easier to defend themselves by *avoiding* such an individual. The advantages of avoidance are obvious: first, your child will be able to think more clearly when he or she sees someone suspicious in the distance (instead of nearby at the last minute); and second, the chances of getting away are better when there is no physical contact.

5. We have also emphasized the importance of character building. The key word here is "building" instead of just "breaking" or "taking apart" or "destroying" or any other such notions that are usually associated with a self-defence course.

We hope to arm your child with a positive attitude by what we have to say in our discussion on Patience. It goes a long way to ensure his or her success not only in this or any other martial arts program but also in school and everyday life.

Respect is another trait that we want our students to have. A lot of the violence in the schools, at home, and elsewhere stems from a lack of respect—from not considering each other as a human being.

6. Of course, your child should know how to repel an attacker once an attack has been launched. We will also deal with that but with the understanding that the information is to be used when there are no choices. Kids have to be made aware that there are choices on the "streets". Instead of going through the trauma involved in a direct confrontation, there are other alternatives such as: ignoring, running, walking away, talking instead of fighting, or recognizing certain signs that spell danger. (A more elaborate discussion on recognizing "danger zones" is given in our topic on "Avoidance".)

7. All our techniques are explained step by step and accompanied with an overflow of photos to give our instructions additional clarity.

8. This first volume is part of our complete system. It contains all the requirements for Level 1 and 2. Our next volume will give an in depth analysis of Level 3 and 4, and our third volume will cover Level 5. (Refer to the section on "Ranking" for more information.)

9. Practical applications are offered. They are "simple" and "effective" for kids in a variety of difficult situations. They are not complete by themselves but are the building blocks for other variations to come.

As we have hinted earlier, **_the information will also benefit the parents_**, so do not let the sudden switch in our style of writing (for the benefit of our younger students) in the following chapters fool you. Once you become familiar with the contents, you can help your child with whatever problems that he or she might have (before they resort to us).

After you turn this page, your son or daughter will be in one of our classes. To make it as real as possible, we have: brought up questions that he or she might actually ask as we go along, took extra time to elaborate on each topic in order to make it as clear as possible, and encouraged the reader to write to us about any difficulties that he or she might have. (We can be reached at the address given in the "Afterword" part of this book.)

We hope you will find our experiment interesting.

Dear Students:

Our aim is to help you learn something about our self-defence program. If you are already taking or have taken some lessons, we do not want to replace what you have learned (unless you are doing something very wrong); instead, we want to add to what you already know.

We also think that the information here will reduce the amount of problems that some of you might have by just attending a self-defence class once a week. If your attendance is less frequent or if you are unable to attend at all, it is an excellent guide for training on your own.

We recognize that there are people with a strong desire to learn the art of self-defence but are unable to take lessons due to certain circumstances. If you happen to have such a problem, it should not stop you if you are persistent. You have to make use of whatever means that are available, and we hope that this book will give you more than a head start.

A Few Things About Us

We want you to know a little bit about us before we begin. We will not bore you with stories about our actual self-defence experiences, the number of degrees that we have (university and otherwise), our martial arts qualifications, achievements, how long we have studied, what we know, who we know, how many tournaments we have fought in (and will be fighting in), how many trophies we won, etc.

Sometimes you will have a better idea of what a person is like by just looking at what he or she does. Here are some pictures of what we do:

Creating a winning team at the
"Canadian Open Kung-fu Championships".

Introducing "SELF-DEFENCE" to the Girl Guides.

Performing a "breaking" demonstration.

Demonstrating a kung-fu "form".

Conducting a seminar at a public school.

Introducing "SELF-DEFENCE" to the Brownies.

Turning a contender into a champion.

Teaching a typical class.

Awarding a black sash and certificate to one of our students

Ranking

Our ranking system is divided into five levels. The information in this book covers everything you need to know up to and including Level 2. Our intermediate manual includes what you have to know for Level 3 and Level 4, and our advance manual contains all the necessary information for Level 5.

Level 1 covers the following techniques:

1. Stances: Close Stance, Open Stance, Front Stance, Drop Knee Stance, Horse Stance.

2. Blocks: Low Block, Thrust Block, Palm Block, High Block.

3. Hand Techniques: Sun Fist, Corkscrew Punch, Reverse Punch, Hammer Fist, Back Fist.

4. Leg Techniques: Front Kick, Roundhouse Kick, Side Kick, Back Kick.

5. Applications: Blocking (Hammer Fist/High Block, Back Fist/Thrust Block, Back Fist/Palm Block, Front Kick/Low Block).

Level 2 covers the following techniques:

1. Hand Techniques: Back Fist and Reverse Punch.
2. Leg Techniques: Double Roundhouse Kick, Spinning Back Kick.
3. Footwork: Cross-Over Side Kick, Hopping Side Kick.
4. Applications: Counter Attack (Thrust Block and Reverse Punch, Low Block and Reverse Punch).
5. Defence Against Strangulation: Spear Hand, Dropping the Bridge, Buddha Clasp Hands.

What Is Self-Defence?

This book is about *SELF-DEFENCE* not *self-defence*.

There is a difference between *SELF-DEFENCE* (in the upper case) and *self-defence* (in the lower case). We are not just teaching you *self-defence* but also *SELF-DEFENCE*. Although we will talk about *self-defence* applications later, do not forget that it is part of *SELF-DEFENCE*.

"What's the difference?" you might ask.

Plenty.

In *self-defence*, you are depending mainly on your physical strength to defend yourself. In *SELF-DEFENCE*, however, you are using your mind as well as your body to defend yourself. *SELF-DEFENCE* also includes backing away, walking away, running, staying put, keeping your distance, and/or thinking before you react.

If you do not make a distinction between *self-defence* and *SELF-DEFENCE* and rely only on brute force, then you will develop the tendency of holding your ground and fight in any situation instead of retreating.

18

"When do I retreat?" you might ask.

Whenever you can. Whenever it is possible.

"Do I back away from someone who is smaller than me?"

Definitely.

"Why?" you are curious to know.

First, you will often be taken by surprise, and you will not have time to scan the area around you to see if you are dealing with more than one person.

Second, he or she may be armed. You may be fast with your fist and your feet, but did you know that there are people who are extremely skillful with knives, clubs, sticks, chains, and other (usual and unusual) weapons? They can perform all sorts of stabbing, slicing, thrusting, whipping, and other techniques that you have never dreamed of. Worst of all, he or she may have a gun.

Third, even if you know for sure that you can easily win the fight, he or she might want to get even. Revenge is a very messy thing to be involved in because it goes on and on and somewhere along the way people lose control.

That is, suppose Fred clobbered Barney because of something that he said, and Barney got even by sneaking up to him one day and whopped him behind the head and ran away. When Fred slugged him in return the next day, Barney got really upset and thought about resorting to other ways to get back at him.

If his fist could not get the job done, then maybe he needs a weapon or the help from some of his friends. Even if Fred is not worry about such threats, he still has to deal with the problem of not knowing *when* it will happen (it always seems that it will happen when he least expects it), *where* it will happen, *what* will happen, and *who* or how many of them will make it happen; and once it happens, he might even forget exactly *why* it happened. If he could not remember, then it must have been something unimportant—something which could have been handled another way.

So contrary to popular opinion, there is no shame in retreating. In fact, it may be the smartest thing to do. The only time you stand your ground and fight is when you have no choice. But when you have a choice to run, you run. When you have a choice to walk away, you walk away. When there is an opportunity for you to back away even when you are right in the thick of things, you back away.

We agree that it is sometimes hard for you to walk away from a fight in front of your friends. Peer pressure, your reputation, and a number of other things are at stake. If you have friends who admire you for fighting but sneer at you and say bad things about you behind you back when you walk away, then are they really your friends? Can you trust that sort of friendship? We will discuss this some more when we get to the subject on "Trust" in the next chapter.

Chapter 1

SELECTED TOPICS

Trust

When you trust someone, you do not have to worry about your safety whenever you are with him or her. If you start to worry, even a little bit, then there is a lack of trust.

"But who do I trust?" you might ask.

That question can best be answered by learning more about who you should not trust. You were probably often reminded, "Watch out for strangers" or "Don't take anything from strangers." Those kinds of advice are very good, but suppose we were to ask you the question, who is a stranger? What would your answer be?

"Someone whom I never met before," you replied.

Yes, that would definitely make him or her a stranger. But what if you had already met that person once or twice? Is he or she still a stranger? What if you had met someone else three or four times? Is that person your friend then? What about a dozen times? You might argue that they are not total strangers. But they are not "totally" your friends either.

How often you see them is not as important as how well you know them. It is possible to meet someone often but not really get to know them. People that you do not know well are your acquaintances. People that you have known for a long time are more likely to be your friends. Friendship takes a long time to develop. Get to know the difference between an acquaintance and a friend.

It's the same thing with trust. Trust also takes a long time to develop. It does not happen overnight. That is why you should be suspicious if a stranger or a person you hardly know asks you to trust him or her. They may not exactly say, "Trust me." They may ask you to go with them in their car or to follow them to their home; but that is the same thing since what they actually want you to do is to completely trust them. We suggest that you **DO NOT**.

We are not saying that you should not trust anyone. We are just saying that you should have a healthy suspicion especially towards strangers. Our definition of a "stranger" includes people that you do not know that well as well as people that you do not know at all.

When a stranger approaches you and starts talking to you as if he or she has known you for a long time, then you should immediately sense that something is wrong. When that happens, remember what we have said in the last chapter: in addition to self-defence, you also have to think about backing away, walking away, running, keeping your distance, and/or thinking before you react.

Avoidance

A lot of people like to start a self-defence course by getting right into the thick of things: the hitting, kicking, and chopping part of it. Although it is true that martial arts can prepare you physically for dangerous situations, the mental side is often totally forgotten, ignored, or not taken serious.

If you depend on your strength alone, you will not get very far. At your age, a big opponent means someone who is really **BIG**. By that we mean he or she could be twice as tall, three times as heavy, and maybe even four times stronger than you. Imagine such a person sneaking up behind you. You probably think that it does not matter how **BIG** he or she is because the first thing that comes to your mind is that you are going to karate chop him or her down to size. But we might as well tell you right now that the odds are still going to be against you even if you know karate, kung fu, or any other type of martial arts.

To make matters worst, notice that we also said that he or she had *snuck up behind you.* Attacks from the rear will give you more problems than attacks from the front. Your reaction will be slower since you are taken by surprise. You cannot see your attacker, so you are forced to fight blind. Once he or she grabs you, there will be no room for you to use your favourite kick because kicks are intended for long range fighting. You may not even get a chance to use your fist even though it is suitable for short and medium range. You might be held so snugly that you cannot even move never mind kicking or punching. However, he or she will have the choice of hitting or strangling you.

So how can you defend against a really **BIG** person who you will not see, who you will have difficulty hitting, and who will probably hit you first?

This is where *avoidance* comes in. We have briefly mentioned one type of avoidance in our discussion on "What is Self-Defence". In that section, we were talking about *avoiding* a confrontation by walking or running away *after* someone *directly* challenges you.

But sometimes you will not be aware of your attacker's presence. He or she will just sneak up to you from behind and "grab" you. In this case, you have to defend yourself by *avoiding* him or her altogether *before* he or she attacks you *indirectly.*

"How can I avoid someone who I can not see?" you might ask.

The most effective way is to know what can happen before it happens by improving, what we called, your "awareness". Let's talk about this for a moment.

Awareness

Being aware of what can possibly happen to you (when you see someone approaching you or when your notice the sudden change in your surroundings) is the first step in preparing yourself.

Moreover, we want you to be especially aware of a certain type of individual who may approach you directly or indirectly: **an abductor**. We will often only refer to this person as a **"he"**, but do not forget that it is also possible for this individual to be a **"she"**.)

An abductor is someone who kidnaps people for different reasons: for money, to harm them, and to do other things to them that are too horrible to talk about. The way that you handle a bully who constantly teases you or wants to pick a fight with you, for example, might not work against somebody who wants to abduct you. An abductor is more of a threat to you, so he has to be dealt with in a different way.

Do not wait for him to make his first move before you try to defend yourself. Like we said before, it is no fun trying to beat someone bigger and stronger than you. Instead, you can be one step ahead of him by practising the following "approaches" (by actually acting them out by yourself or with a partner and by going through them in your mind):

(A) The Direct Approach

When someone approaches you *directly*, you are able to see and hear him. Go over the following examples of how an abductor behaves when he approaches you directly so that you will be able to immediately recognize and avoid him:

√   Be suspicious of anyone who acts suspiciously. For example, instead of talking to you, a person may gradually move closer and closer to you. He may stop and glance around and then come even closer. That person may stop again and glance around some more...like a shoplifter who wants to steal something. He will glance to the left and then to the right and then to the rear and then maybe back to the right and then to the left... What you have to do in this case is to move farther and farther away. Leave the area, and run if you have to.

√   Do not trust strangers who try to carry on a conversation with you. They might eventually try to trick you into going somewhere with them, and they have different ways of doing it. For instance, he may say that your mom told you to go with him. The stranger may even call you by your name to prove that he knows your mom. There may be other kids in the car that you know, and the stranger will tell you that even their moms said that it is OK. But if your mom did not mention to you about going with another person, don't go.

√   Do not respond to strangers who ask for your name, address, phone number, or any other personal information.

√   Turn down anything that a stranger gives you regardless of how much he tempts you. Keep in mind that it may not be easy for you to say NO if he knows your weaknesses and offers you something which is difficult to resist.

√   Do not open your door to strangers. They may pretend to be couriers, service people, or someone pretending to be in trouble. If they ask you for the use of your phone, tell them that you'll make the call instead.

(B) The Indirect Approach

When an abductor approaches you *indirectly*, he is hidden from view, and it is up to you to see and/or hear him. Unlike the direct approach, he will just "grab" you without uttering a word.

Let go back to the question that you have asked in the last section: "How can I avoid someone who I can not see?"

This problem can be dealt with by knowing your surroundings and being able to identify the places where such a person is usually found. They are usually dark, quiet, clutter, well hidden, out of the way, or any combination of such conditions that keep him or her from being seen.

One way to heightening your awareness of your surroundings is to get into the habit of recognizing certain "danger zones". A danger zone will not be marked "Danger Zone". You will not find any signs like that because those places are not dangerous to everybody—only to you. Let's take a look at some of them.

Picture #1 is pretty scary, we agree. The abandoned building has all the stuff that he likes; it is quiet, it's in the middle of nowhere, it is dark inside, and it's partly shaded and hidden by the trees outside.

Picture #2 is not as bad as picture #1, but it is bad enough. Although the parking lot is not hidden from view, it is isolated (in the middle of nowhere), and it is quiet (there is nobody around). It's true that there are no suspicious people around, but someone driving a vehicle can go in and out of there faster than you think.

Picture 1

Picture 2

Picture #3 looks like a nice place. But would you believe that it is almost as bad as picture #1 and worst than picture #2? It is not a good idea to spend a lot of time there by yourself. If you take a closer look, you will find that the playground is just as isolated (in the middle of nowhere) and just as quiet and lonely (there is nobody around) as picture #2. What makes it worst than picture #2 are those dark trees in the background. They make a good hiding spot for anyone who wants to harm you.

Picture #4 seems to be OK. In fact, it seems to be the best picture of them all, but it is not. Avoid taking that path by yourself, and don't even think about hanging around there. It is almost as bad as picture #1 and worst than picture #2; and it is just as bad as (or maybe even worst than) picture #3. Why?

Before you answer, we want you to remember something about those pictures. It is obvious that you should avoid picture #1. Picture #2 might not be so obvious, and picture #3 and #4 might even be less obvious. Sometimes you have to look past the nice things (the beautiful trees, colourful flowers, freshly cut grass, etc.) and the enjoyable things that you like to do (playing on the slide, splashing away at the drinking fountain, bouncing the ball off the wall, etc.) before you can be aware of the unattractive things (the quietness, loneliness, darkness, etc.).

So go over the pictures again and pick out those "unattractive things". Keep doing it until you can see them at a glance. You are training your sixth sense or your "Third Eye" to automatically warn you whenever any of them appears on the "street"— even if it was not that obvious at first. It is normal to forgot about your "Third Eye" since you can not think about it all the time, but it will still behave like a sixth sense to alert you of any possible danger.

That is the first warning you will get when you are alone, and it is the most important. It is a distant warning signal—like a lighthouse redirecting ships that are coming into its path. It is

Picture 3

Picture 4

better to be aware of a "danger zone" first before you see some-one suspicious because you are farther away, and that makes it easier to avoid him (or her).

Simplicity and Effectiveness

"But what would I do if I was too tired or too busy to be aware of my surroundings and was not able to avoid him?" you might ask.

Then you would have to try your best to physically defend yourself. What we are saying up to this point is that you should not wait for the worst to happen first and then decide to do some-thing about it. That is not what we mean by "SELF-DEFENCE".

People often forget that there is a choice between avoiding a situation and engaging in one. Learn to avoid a situation first. That would save you the trouble of having to defend yourself. Again, keep in mind that it can be a lot of "trouble" if you were taken by surprise by somebody who is **BIG**.

However, when you do not have a choice, then you will have to do whatever it takes to deal with the situation. That means: you have to apply the right technique, or you may have to apply several different techniques, or you may have to apply the same technique more than once. In order for you to do that, you have to keep them *simple*.

A lot of students are attracted by the fancy kicks that whirls and twirls in the air like the way they are done on TV and in the movies. We will cover some of those moves later. At this stage, however, we want you to learn certain things that are better suited for your age, height, and built.

If we demonstrate a simple technique, some of you might say, "What? That's it? That's all there is to it?"

No. Not exactly. Our basic techniques are not only simple; they are also *effective*. That means you can cause serious damage when you do them right. That makes a lot of difference. If a technique is simple but not effective, it will not work no matter how much you practise it.

Even more important, do not think that if a technique is difficult to perform, it must be effective. Most of the fancy techniques that involves leaping and spinning are not effective because they will not work in a real situation.

Before we move on to something else, there are just a few more topics that we want to discuss with you: patience, respect, and safety. Those topics relate the way you think (your mind) to the way you practise the art of self-defence (your body).

Patience

Usually it is very easy for you to learn and make a lot of progress in the beginning (at our school or at any other martial arts school); but when your lessons get harder, you might start to slow down. You might be stuck for months trying to do a single technique. You might keep forgetting certain steps in a particular set of movement (even after you have done it hundreds of times). You might find other students a rank ahead of you (even though you have started earlier), and you might even fail your tests again for the fourth time in a row. Or was it the fifth? You are not sure. You have lost count. Anyway, you might get so discourage that thoughts of quitting will start creeping into your mind.

But before you decide to do that, remember: there are no deadlines to meet when you are learning self-defence—especially SELF-DEFENCE. (If you forgot the difference between them, go over again the section on "What is Self-Defence".) It is better to take your time to do things right, and that means sticking with it until it is done properly. That is hard to do sometimes not just in self-defence, but also in anything else that requires a bit of work.

Sticking with it means never giving up. There are a lot of talented people who never achieve what they are capable of doing because they gave up too soon. You see...talent alone is not enough. Sometimes it might even get in the way. That often happens when a person is very good at what he or she does and thinks that practise and hard work is not necessary in his or her case.

That individual will often learn very quickly in the beginning but will tend to lag behind later when the going gets tough because he or she is missing one other important quality besides talent: patience. Remember:

It is not surprising for a patience person without a lot of talent to eventually catch up with a talented person without a lot of patience.

The following are some people who are able to accomplish what they wanted to do because they were able to stick with it:

You probably all have heard of Dr. Seuss, the author of "The Cat in the Hat" line of books. Did you know that his first book was rejected twenty-three times. But he never gave up. Because of his persistence, he is one of the world's most popular children's author. His books have sold millions of copies all over the world.

"Yeah, but I have problems..." you might say.

What problems? Physical problems? Well, let us tell you about two outstanding athletes whose physical problems did not stop them from doing what they want to do:

In 1966, Bill Wallace suffered torn ligaments in his right knee while studying judo. When he began training in karate months later, he found that he could not use his right leg. Although he only kicks with his left leg, he was still able to win twenty-three professional fights without a loss.

Bruce Lee was only 5 feet 6 1/2 inches. He was nearsighted, and one of his leg was slightly longer than the other. But he still managed to become a legend in martial arts. He wrote several books and made a number of movies.

"But they are smart," you might add.

Then consider some of these people:

Thomas Edison never even finished grade school but that did not stop him from inventing the electric light, the phonograph, motion pictures, and a long list of other inventions.

Steven Spielberg's high-school grades were so poor that he was unable to get into any major film school. He had to bluff his way into movie studios and learn his craft the hard way. Now he is a famous director with successful movies like Close Encounters of the Third Kind, E.T., Indiana Jones, Empire of the Sun, Jurassic Park, Schindler's List, etc.

So if you did not pass our test or a test your instructor gave you, the *real test* is the question: are you going to stick with it or are you going to give up? (This applies not only to martial arts, but also to any difficult task that you are up against.)

Respect

Sometimes your learning can also be interrupted by a lack of respect as well as a lack of patience.

Respect means conducting yourself properly. There are two types of respect: respect for yourself and respect for others. Both are important.

If you respect yourself, you want to do the best you can to improve both your mind and body. You do not want to abuse yourself mentally and physically by adopting bad habits like smoking, drinking, and/or taking drugs.

It is from respecting yourself that you will get to know what you have to do to take care of yourself. When it comes to respecting others, you will do the same thing for them. If you do not treat yourself with care, then most likely you will not treat others with care.

"Why should I go out of my way to treat others like that?" you might ask.

Because people will treat you the same way as you treat them. If you do not respect them, do not expect them to respect you. To put this another way, you have to treat others like the way you would like to be treated. So one way to gain respect is to show some first, and you have to get into the habit of showing it all the time.

If you treat your classmates in a fair and decent way when the instructor is around but abuse and bully them when they are by themselves, you are only pretending to be respectful. You may not even be aware that you are doing it if you have done it for so long that you don't give it a second thought. Then when you do decide to treat them fairly, you might wonder why you don't get the same treatment in return. The answer is that you have to show your respect all the time instead of just some of the time. People have a tendency to remember how disrespectful you were even if you have shown it just once.

Here are some examples of displaying a lack of respect in class: not listening or doing what the instructor tells you to do, being constantly late, bullying and mistreating your fellow students, and using foul language.

Maybe you are not aware of it, but if you continue to be disrespectful to someone, what you are really saying is that you *don't care about that person.* And that is exactly how he or she will treat you.

Safety

So far, we have been talking about doing things safe on the "street". We also want you to do things safe when you are training indoors on your own or with a partner.

In either case, you have to keep your eyes "open". It is not that hard. You do it every day. When you go out for a walk, for example, you avoid objects that are in your way with hardly any effort. It comes naturally. Keeping your eyes "open" does not take up too much of your conscious mind. With practise, you can improve this sixth sense. We have told you how to do that outside in our discussion about improving your "awareness". Now you have to do the same thing indoors.

When you are going through a particular technique for the first time, it is very important to ask yourself if it is safe and if it feels right. If you do not think that it is safe, then stop and take some time to find out why.

Check to see if you are doing anything wrong. Know all the steps involved by going through each movement slowly at first. If you rush through them in a hurry, you might skip a step and not be aware of it until much later. By then, the mistake will be harder to correct; or worst, it might cause serious injuries.

Once you are sure that you are doing it right (according to the way that you were instructed to do it), repeat it gradually. Do not push yourself to the point of exhaustion.

Also pay attention to your surroundings. Is the floor slippery? Are there sharp edges nearby? Are there things in your way? Are there small objects on the floor? Are your classmates too close to you? (When you practise with a partner, watch out for his or her safety as well as yours.)

In other words, you have to watch for anything out of the ordinary. You will become skillful in doing that by becoming aware of what is suppose to be "ordinary" in the first place. You can achieve that by:

1. Knowing the correct steps involved in a technique.

2. Know what your surroundings are suppose to be like. For example: Are the tables and chairs out of the way? Is the floor clean? Are the mats arranged properly?

Once you are completely satisfy with your surroundings, let's start with some very interesting exercises.

Chapter 2

EXERCISING

Points to Remember:

There are several reasons why you have to exercise:

1. To prevent being overweight. Too much weight can cause a lot of problems: it will make you breathe harder, put pressure on your joints, and keep you from moving fast.

2. To increase flexibility.

3. To build stronger muscles.

4. To prepare your body for hard work.

A word of caution: warm up first with some exercise like those mentioned in the sections on warming up before you stretch. Do not stretch before you warm up.

"Why can't I stretch first?" you might ask.

If you hold an icicle in your hand and try to bend it, what happens? That's right. It breaks. When you are cold, (especially in the winter when the temperature is often in the subzero region), you muscles will become stiff; and if you force a stretch, you will hurt yourself. So it is important to warm up first before you stretch or do certain movements that require full extension of your muscles.

Body Parts

Throughout the book, different parts of the body will be mentioned. You can refer to them on the diagrams we have labelled below and on the next page.

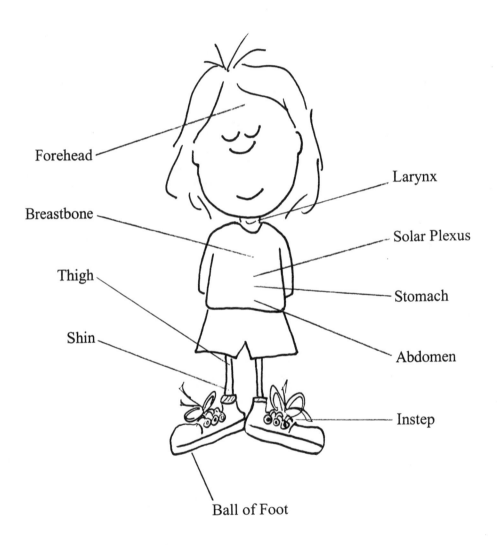

Forehead

Larynx

Breastbone

Solar Plexus

Thigh

Stomach

Shin

Abdomen

Instep

Ball of Foot

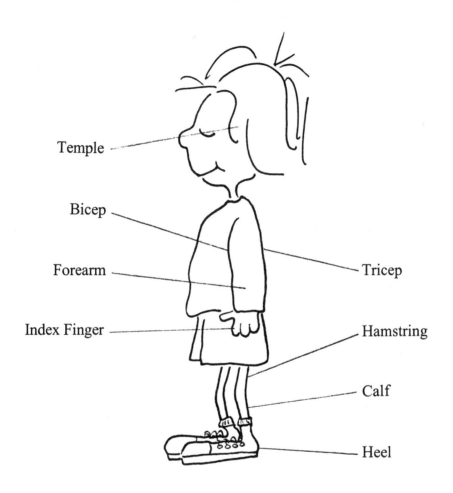

Temple

Bicep

Forearm

Index Finger

Tricep

Hamstring

Calf

Heel

Joint Warm Up

"Joint warm ups" are done first to allow different parts of your body to rotate easier. When you are doing these exercises, you are not stretching any major muscle; you are only loosening your joints and the muscles that surround them. Let's start with the upper joints of your body and work down:

1. Rotate your head to the left and look past your left shoulder. Then turn to the right and look past your right shoulder, etc. See figures 1 and 2.

2. Bend your head sideways until your left ear comes close to your left shoulder as in figure 3. Then bend it sideways to the right until your right ear comes close to your right shoulder as in figure 4. Keep facing straight ahead as you repeat the movements.

3. Tilt your head downwards, as in figure 5, and then straighten it up. Then tilt it down again, etc.

4. Push your chin forward and then allow it to bounce back. Then push it forward again, etc. Your head will bob back and forth like a chicken. See figures 6 and 7.

5. Hold your left arm across your body and wrap your right arm up against your left elbow as in figure 8. Then pull your right arm in towards you. You should be able to feel the stretch in your left shoulder. Repeat the same movements on the opposite side as in figure 9.

6. Hold your left arm up and allow the upper arm to drop behind your back. Then reach behind your head with your right hand and grab your left elbow and pull downwards as in figure 10. Repeat this exercise on the opposite side as in figure 11.

7. Dangle your arms loosely by your side and relax. See

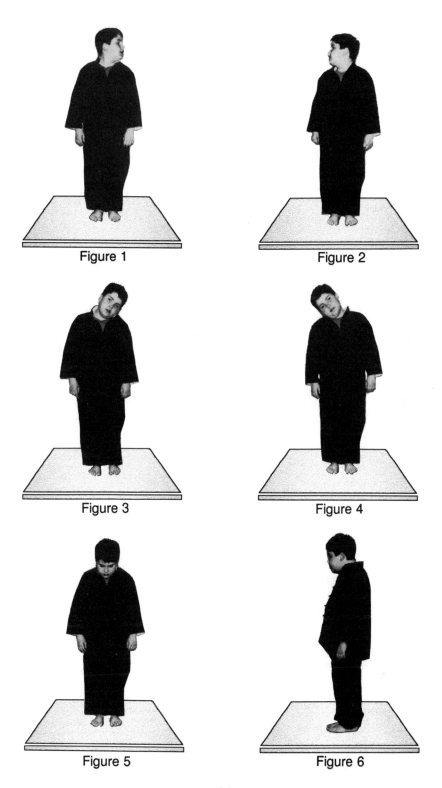

Figure 1

Figure 2

Figure 3

Figure 4

Figure 5

Figure 6

41

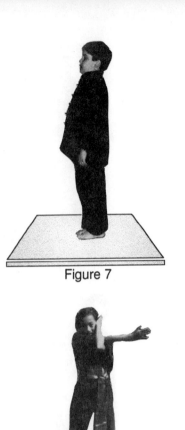

Figure 7

Figure 8

Figure 9

Figure 10

Figure 11

Figure 12

figure 12. Then hunch your shoulders as in figure 13. Hold them in that position for a few seconds before you let them drop. Then hunch them again, etc.

8. Join the front knuckles of your fists and bring them up to your chest as in figure 14. While keeping your toes pointing straight ahead, turn your body to your left as far as you can. Then turn to your right, etc. See figures 15 and 16.

9. Place your hands on your hips. You are facing the front, and your toes are pointing straight ahead as in figure 17. Start rotating your upper body clockwise by leaning to your left as in figure 18. Then turn and lean backwards as in figure 19, Continue turning and lean to the right as in figure 20. Finally turn and lean forward as in figure 21. Then start the whole process over again.

10. Bend both of your knees forward and place the palms of your hands on top of them as in figure 22. Rotate your knees to the left and use your hands to guide them as in figure 23. Keep turning them towards the back until your legs straighten up as in figure 24. Continue circling and bend your knees to the right as in figure 25. From that position, start over again by rotating them to the left, etc.

11. Reach down with your right hand and grab your left ankle. Bend your foot sideways until only the outer edge is touching the floor. Gradually press down with your right hand and slowly shift some of your body weight to the left. Avoid putting too much pressure against your ankle. See figure 26. Repeat the exercise on your right foot as in figure 27.

12. Turn to your left and rest the instep of your right foot against the floor. Apply steady pressure by lowering your knees. You will feel the stretch in your ankle. See figure 28. Do not put too much weight onto it all at once. Turn to the other side and repeat the same movements.

Figure 13

Figure 14

Figure 15

Figure 16

Figure 17

Figure 18

Figure 19

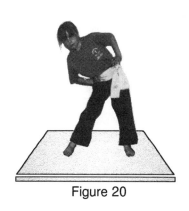

Figure 20

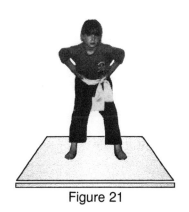

Figure 21

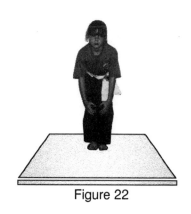

Figure 22

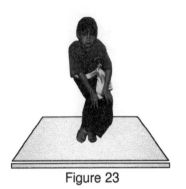

Figure 23

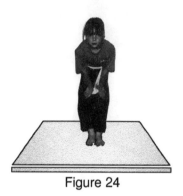

Figure 24

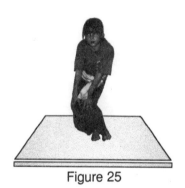

Figure 25

Figure 26

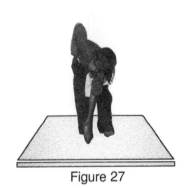

Figure 27

Figure 28

Full Warm Up

After you have done your joint warm up, you are now ready for a full warm up. The following are some exercises to give your larger muscles a workout:

(A) Skipping: Skipping helps you build endurance and co-ordination. Choose a rope which is not too long or too short and try some of the following drills:

1. Skip up and down with both feet at a steady rhythm.

2. When you become used to that, try to skip continuously on just one foot while you keep the other foot off the floor. See figure 29.

3. Then you can try to skipping on each foot in turn. Let's start by raising your right leg off the floor and skip on your left supporting leg as in figure 30. On the way down, you are going to land on your right leg and raise your left leg at the same time as in figure 31. Then skip on your right leg and come down and land on your left, etc. Do not jump up too high off your supporting leg. You want to be able to clear the floor just enough for the rope to pass through. When you can do it smoothly, it will appear as if though you are jogging while you are skipping.

(B) Jumping Jacks: This is a good exercise to help you build endurance. With your arms by your sides and your feet together as in figure 32, jump up and begin raising both your arms over your head and spreading your feet apart as in figure 33. Your arms should be fully extended with your hands clapped together by the time you land as in figure 34. Then jump up again and start to bring both your arms down and your feet together while you are in the air as in figure 35. By the time you land, your arms should be by your side and your feet are together as in figure 36. From this position, repeat the whole movement again.

Figure 29

Figure 30

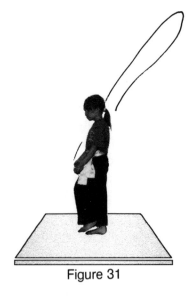

Figure 31

Figure 32

Figure 33

Figure 34

Figure 35

Figure 36

(C) Push ups: Start by lying on your stomach and look straight ahead. Place the palm of your hands on the floor close to your body. Keep both your lower arms vertical and shoulder width apart. Your legs are together and balanced on your toes. See figure 37. Push yourself up. Make sure you extend your arms fully. Do not allow your lower back to sag. You are still looking forward. See figure 38. When you go down again, stop when you are only inches from the floor and push yourself right back up as in figure 39. The muscles used in push-ups are the triceps, forearm, and shoulder. Go through the full range of motion so that those muscles will have a chance to be fully strengthen. That is, go all the way down (until you are only inches away from the floor) and all the way up.

(D) Sit-ups: Here are a few sit-ups you can try:

1. The first type of sit-up that you will do is called a "banana roll". Start by placing your hands across your chest and lie only on your lower back with your legs raised as in figure 40. (Do not sit on your tail bone.) Then lower your legs to the floor and sit straight up as in figure 41. Next, roll backwards and raise your legs until your lower back is touching the floor again. From that position, lower your legs and sit up again, etc.

2. Another type of sit-up is an inverted form of toe touching. Start by lying down with your left arm stretched out behind you on the ground. Lift your right leg up while you raise your body off the floor to touch the toes of your right foot with your left hand. See figures 42 and 43. Repeat the movements on the opposite side, etc.

3. Another variation of the single toe touch sit-up is the double toe touch. Lie on your back with both your legs raised up towards the ceiling. Rest them against the wall for support. Your arms are stretched out pointing towards the ceiling as in figure 44. Then raise your body off the floor and reach for your toes.

Figure 37

Figure 38

Figure 39

Figure 40

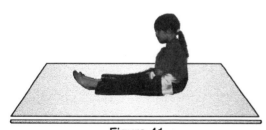

Figure 41

Figure 42

Stretching

Stretching will improve your flexibility and prevent injuries. When you are flexible, less effort is needed to do certain tech niques because you are less stiff. You will perform those movements easier and faster.

Do your stretches slowly at first in case you have not totally warmed up. If you have never done any stretching before, do not force yourself beyond the point where you can not stretch any farther. Try to hold your stretch for thirty seconds or longer instead of constantly stretching and unstretching.

It's a good idea to ask your mom or dad to help you keep your balance and/or to apply steady pressure when you attempt some of the more difficult stretches. Do not worry if you cannot complete them like the way they are done in the photographs. It takes a lot of practise.

1. A good way to stretch your hamstrings and calves is shown in figure 45. While you are sitting on the ground, your legs are together and straightened out in front of you. Reach and grab the bottom of your left and right feet with each of your hands. Bring your body forward until your chest comes close to your knees. When you become more flexible, you may actually touch your knees. (If you just want to stretch your hamstrings and not your calves, bend your knees slightly.)

2. Another way you can stretch your hamstrings is shown in figure 46. From a seated position, bend your right leg and draw it towards you while keeping your right foot flat on the ground. Your left leg is outstretched with the toes pointing straight up. Grab the bottom of your left foot with both hands while you try to bring your chin over your left knee. Gradually reach out farther as you become more flexible. Try the same exercise on your other leg as in figure 47.

Figure 43

Figure 44

Figure 45

Figure 46

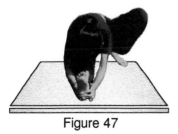

Figure 47

Figure 48

3. Figure 48 is a good example of a front split from a standing position. Widen your open stance as much as possible. Your toes are pointing straight ahead. Then slowly lower yourself to the ground. Place your hands on the floor for support.

4. From position (3) above, roll your legs backwards until your toes point up. Then sit down. With your legs the same width apart, reach out as far as possible with both your hands. As you gain flexibility, touch the floor with both of your elbows. See figure 49.

5. From position (4) above, you can also go into a side split as in figure 50. Turn to your right and point the toes of your right foot forward, and rest the instep of your rear foot on the ground. Keep your right knee facing up. It is important to keep the knee of the rear leg turned down instead of to the side. This will take a lot of pressure off that joint. Use your hands for support. Turn to your left and repeat the same stretch.

6. From a split in the seated position as in (4), grab the bottom of the inside part of your left and right heels with each of your hands. Then sit back and balance yourself in a V position while you steadily push your legs farther apart. See figure 51.

7. From a standing position, grab the outside edge of your left foot with your right hand as in figure 52. Then straighten the left leg out in front of you while you maintain your grip. See figure 53. Repeat the same movements with your right leg as in figure 54 and 55.

8. From a standing position, place the heel of your right foot against the palm of your right hand. Extend and raise your right leg as high as possible. Use your hand as support. See figure 56. Try the same stretch with your left leg.

Figure 49

Figure 50

Figure 51

Figure 52

Figure 53

Figure 54

Figure 55

Figure 56

Chapter 3

STANCES

Points to Remember:

The word "stance" refer to the way you stand when you practise martial arts. The different stances in this chapter will help you improve your balance and strengthen your legs. Here are some things to keep in mind while you try them:

1. Start by placing both of your fists by the sides of your chest as in figure 57. The back of both fists should be facing down towards the floor with the thumbs facing up.

2. Go back to figure 57 again, and you will notice that both of the fists are not resting on the hips because the forearms would then be tilted (in relation to the ground). Hold your fists up high near your chest to keep your forearms parallel to the floor.

3. In figure 57, also note that the front of both fists are even with the front of the body.

4. The elbows are not flapping out but are tucked in against your sides. They are in line with the front of your fists. Again, see figure 57.

5. Whatever stance you are in, be sure to pay close attention to your posture. If possible, check in front of a mirror to make sure that your head is not tilted, that your body is not leaning too much to either side, and that you are not putting more weight on one leg than the other.

6. Also, turn sideways and check in the mirror to make sure that your back is straight and that you are not leaning forward or backwards.

7. One way to spot any problem is to draw an imaginary line down through the centre of your body. Try to visualize this line from the front (as in figure 58) and from the side (as in figure 59) when you are in front of a mirror. Do not lean away from that line.

Bad posture and martial arts do not go together. Now is the time to do something about it. The longer you practise with a bad posture, the harder it will be for you to make any corrections later.

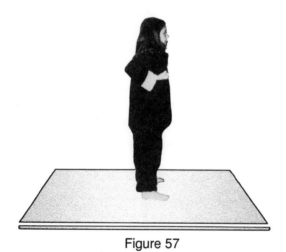

Figure 57

Figure 58

Figure 59

Close Stance

The closed stance is not a fighting stance. It is used mainly for bowing. Perform the close stance by:

1. Bring your feet together and place your fists against your sides. See figure 60.

2. Make good eye contact by looking straight ahead instead of downwards or off to the side.

3. Stand straight. Make sure that you have a good posture.

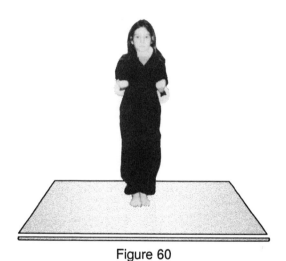

Figure 60

Open Stance

Your open stance is used when you are practising hand techniques and when you are doing joint warm ups. Go into an open stance by following these steps:

1. From the close stance with your fists against your sides as in figure 60, open your stance by stepping out to the side with your right foot for example.

2. The stance is about as wide as your shoulders. Make any necessary adjustment if yours is wider or narrower than that. Later you should be able to do it with a single step without any adjustment. See figure 61.

3. Check your posture.

Figure 61

Front Stance

The front stance is also called a "bow stance" or "fighting stance". It is used when you are practising your hand or leg techniques. Perform the front stance by following these steps:

1. From a close stance with your fists against your sides as in figure 62, go into an open stance as in figure 63.

2. Then take a step forward with your left foot, and bend the left knee at the same time. Do not lean forward. It is a good exercise to hold this position for a few minutes. See figure 64.

3. Try to keep the knee of your leading leg directly over the big toe. As your legs get stronger lower your stance more by taking a longer step.

4. The rear leg is kept straight.

5. The rear foot is at 45 degrees instead of pointing straight ahead or to the side. Your front foot points in the same direction as your rear foot.

6. Notice that the rear leg is not directly behind the front leg. Its width is the same as the open stance.

7. Check your posture.

8. Switch your stance by going back into an open stance and stepping forward with your other foot. Go through steps 2 to 7 again.

Figure 62

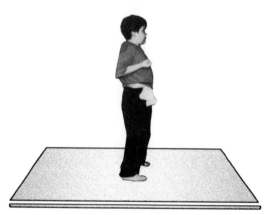

Figure 63

Figure 64

Drop Knee Stance

The drop knee stance allows you to get low without losing your balance. It is used to change the direction of your attack and/or to avoid your opponent's attack. Go through the following steps when you attempt it:

1. You are in a right front stance with your fists by your sides as in figure 65.

2. Without changing the width of the stance, bend your rear leg until you are on the ball of your foot and your knee is in line with your shoulder. See figure 66.

3. Check your posture. Practise the above movement in a left front stance also.

Figure 65

Figure 66

Horse Stance

The horse stance is used to strengthen the thighs and to improve your balance. It is called a horse stance because it looks as if though you are riding a horse. Sometimes it is also called a "sumo stance". The follow steps will guide you in opening this stance:

1. From the close stance with your fists against your sides as in figure 67, spread the toes of both your feet outward as far as possible. Your heels are still touching each other. See figure 68. Then**...**

2. ...from that position, spread your heels outward as far as possible. Your toes will then be pointing towards each other as in figure 69. Then**...**

3. ...from there, again spread your toes outwards as far as possible. Your heels will then be pointing towards each other as in figure 70. Then**...**

4. ...when you have gotten that far, shift your heels out until your toes point straight ahead (instead of at an angle as in the other steps). See figure 71. That is the width of your horse stance. Keep that width in mind. As you become familiar with this stance, you should be able to go into it with a single step (like going into an open stance) without measuring it first as in the above steps.

5. Lower your stance until your knees are over your toes. See figure 72.

6. Be sure to check your posture. Keep your back straight and do not lean forward.

7. If you can not hold this stance too long, get up altogether, take a rest, and start all over again rather than getting into the

Figure 67

Figure 68

Figure 69

Figure 70

Figure 71

Figure 72

habit of gradually straightening up and holding the stance at the wrong height. Try to be in a *proper* horse stance for as long as you can. There are martial artists who can hold this stance steady for hours at a time, but do not push yourself to such extremes at first. It will be enough of a challenge for you to try to hold it for two minutes. That is the length of time you should be aiming for at this level.

8. If your legs shake, let them shake. With enough practise, the shaking will gradually stop.

9. Then try to go lower until your seat is in line with your knees. (Your legs will start shaking again, and you have to strengthen them some more.)

Chapter 4

BLOCKING

Points to Remember:

When you try to catch a baseball that has been hit very hard, you would want to get your glove and your body in front of it to keep it from getting by you. Now imagine a harder object ten times larger than a baseball coming directly towards you at the same speed. Your approach would be a lot different. You would not even think of stopping it. Most likely, you would want to get out of the way. (We will discuss the footwork involved in our next manual.)

Another option is to slow it down and/or to redirect it by just touching a part of it. It's like how a hockey player deflects a hard shot by his team mate; he would redirect it towards the net by making light contact with his stick.

You should perform your blocks the same way instead of "winding up" your blocking arm (by clenching your fist and drawing your arm back before slamming it into the path of an oncoming punch or kick with all your strength). Besides hurting yourself, going through all those steps (tightening up, withdrawing your arm, and using a lot of force) will only delay your reaction.

We suggest that you keep the following things in mind instead:

1. Start your blocks right from where your hand is positioned;

in this case, from the ready position. Most people like to draw their arm back and tighten up for extra power, but a lot of power is not necessary to deflect a punch or kick.

2. Your arm should be relax enough to allow you to react like a whip. That is how you gain speed.

3. Do not "lock up" your arm by fully extending your block. Keep your elbow slightly bent. (Refer to the section on "Ready Position" and "Low Block" for more information.)

4. Do not stoop and reach out when you block.

5. When you attempt to block an extremely powerful kick, you might have to start moving *slightly* away from the kick just before you block; the movement of your body will absorb some of the force. We will discuss the footwork involved in the next volume. For now, just practise leaning away without using any footwork.

6. It is very important to immediately get your hand back to your "ready position" after you block.

Ready Position

You must be in the proper defensive position before you can perform any technique to defend yourself. Figure 73 is a typical ready position in a left front stance. The hand in front is called the "leading hand" (or feeling hand) and the one behind it is called the "reserve hand" (or emergency hand). Also notice that:

1. The gap between your hands share a common centre as in figure 74, and that common centre is at the same level as your centre.

"Where is my centre?" you might ask.

71

To find it, draw two imaginary lines: one straight down the middle of your body and another across your chest; the point at where those lines cross is your centre. See figure 75. The hands should not be too far away from the vertical line nor should they be too far above or below the horizontal line.

2. Your arms should not be straight. Get into the habit of keeping them slightly bent at the elbows. That will allows you to absorb the force from a punch or kick when you block. But the arms should not be bent too much; otherwise, you will end up covering more distance between you and your target, and your blocks and punches will be late.

3. The elbows are tucked and pointed down instead of flapping outwards. That will improve your defence by closing off some of the space where a kick or punch can enter. It will also add more power to your punch; you will get more support by lining up your body behind your arm.

4. Avoid spreading your fingers apart. Keep them closed and pointing towards your target. Do not hold them rigid. It will tend to tighten up your arm as well. A stiff arm will prevent you from "lashing" out when you block or punch.

Figure 73

Figure 74

Figure 75

Low Block

The low block is mainly used against kicks and punches that come under your guard. Normally you would use the "leading hand" from the ready position, but you can also use the "reserve hand" if a kick or punch is coming towards you at an angle that is hard for your "leading hand" to reach. Here's how to perform the low block:

1. From the ready position as in figure 76, meet the kick or punch with the "leading hand". It is not done with a chop; it is more of a pressing motion. *Drop* your hand straight down from your ready position (instead of drawing it back and swinging it down). See figure 77.

2. To avoid blocking too close or too far away, keep your arm at an angle of about 45 degrees away from your body.

3. Make contact with your palm not your fingers. Point your fingers to the side to avoid jamming them and to expose your palm to meet the oncoming kick or punch. See figure 78.

4. Keep the arm slightly bent at the elbow as in figure 78. That will allow you to quickly raise your hand back up into the ready position after you have made contact—as if though you had touched a red hot object.

"Why?" you may ask.

Well, suppose that a very powerful front kick was thrown directly at you. A person's leg is stronger than your arm, so the force delivered by your opponent's kick is more powerful than the force from your blocking arm. Failing to withdraw your hand at the right moment will increase the chance of injury. You will make matters worst if you had also straightened out or "locked up" your arm instead of keeping it slightly bent.

By retrieving your hand immediately and by keeping it slightly bent, you are absorbing some of that excess force. Remember, what you want to do is to slow down or deflect the kick instead of trying to stop it.

As we have mentioned earlier, you might even have to start leaning *slightly* away just before you make contact in order to absorb some of the force; but avoid losing your balance by leaning back too far.

5. Go back to your ready position immediately after you have completed the block. (Refer to the chapter on "Applications" for more information.)

6. Go through the above steps with your "reserve hand" also.

Figure 76

Figure 77

Figure 78

Figure 79

Figure 80

Thrust Block

Use the thrust block against strikes at or near the level of your guarding hand. Let's go through this block step by step:

1. From the ready position as in figure 79, thrust your "leading hand" out in front of you with the palm facing up and horizontal to the ground. It is like holding a tray in your hand. Keep your fingers close and lock your thumb so that they will not get jammed. See figure 80.

2. Your arm is still slightly bent at the elbows. Do not straighten out your arm.

3. Your hand and your lower arm should be in line with your centre since you have thrusted your arm out ahead of you instead of swinging it to the side.

4. The contact point could be the thumb side or the top of your forearm depending on where the strike is coming from.

5. If you are blocking a powerful kick with this block, try not to catch the kick on the bony part (on the thumb side) of your forearm. A person's leg is more powerful than your arm, so you have to adjust your arm (and your body) a bit to catch his kick on the flat side (or the top) of your forearm. As we have mentioned in the section on "Points to Remember", you might even have to start leaning *slightly* away from the kick just before you make contact in order to absorb some of the force. Avoid losing your balance by leaning back too much.

6. Immediately go back into the ready position after you have completed the block. (Refer to the chapter on Applications for more information.)

7. Practise this block with your "reserve hand" also.

Palm Block

Like the thrust block, the palm block can also be used against punches or kicks coming at or near the level of your guarding hand. Here's how it's done:

1. From your ready position as in figure 81, deflect the punch or kick with the palm of your "reserve hand" by pushing it across your body as in figure 82.

2. Do not block too close to your body. If you allow a strike to come too close to you, it is very difficult to block it. Keep your fingers pointing up and block diagonally across with your arm at an angle of about 45 degree from your body.

3. Avoid blocking with your fingers. A powerful punch or kick can jam them.

4. Do not draw your hand back before blocking. It is more of a push than a slap.

5. Avoid committing too much on your push. If you use excessive effort, you might end up too far away from your centre; and it will be very difficult to recover fast enough if you miss the block. To make things worst, you might also be off balance.

6. Do not "lock up" your arm after you block.

7. Again, if you are blocking a powerful kick, you might have to start leaning *slightly* away from the kick just before you make contact in order to absorb some of the force. Avoid the habit of leaning back too much. Besides losing your balance, your counter attack (which we will discuss in Chapter 8) will have to cover more distance. This applies to all blocks—but especially to the palm block because of its reach.

8. Immediately return to the ready position after you have completed the block. (Refer to the chapter on "Applications" for more information.)

9. Go through the above steps with your "leading hand" also.

Figure 81

Figure 82

High Block

Use the high block to deflect strikes coming at you above your guard. Perform the block as follows:

1. From the ready position as in figure 83, turn the palm of your "leading hand" out away from your body while raising it at the same time above your forehead as in figure 84. Be sure to keep your arm at a 45 degrees angle in order to deflect an attack.

2. For a strike coming directly overhead, the wrist of your blocking arm (instead of your palm) should line up with the imaginary line drawn vertically through your centre.

3. The contact point is your forearm.

4. Go back to your ready position immediately after you completed the block. (Refer to the chapter on Applications for more information.)

5. Practise this block with your "reserve hand" also.

Figure 83

Figure 84

Chapter 5

PUNCHING

Points to Remember:

Keep the following points in mind when you punch:

1. Always have an imaginary target in front of you when you are training by yourself.

2. Before you learn about the different types of punches, you should first know how to make a fist. There are two ways to do it: the first way is shown in figure 85 with the thumb across the bottom of the index and middle finger, and the other way is shown in figure 86 with the thumb pressing against the side of the index finger.

3. The fist should always be in a straight line with the forearm when you make contact with a target.

4. Relax before you punch. Your arms will then be as flexible as a whip instead of being stiff like a piece of board. Tighten your fist only at the moment of impact. A tightly clenched fist before delivery will tend to tighten the arm as well, and that will slow down your punch.

5. It is not necessary to throw a punch with all your strength (especially if you are not hitting against something). If you keep practising that way, you can injure your joints since there is nothing to absorb the force of your punch. Even if you are hitting against something that offers some resistance, it is still not necessary to punch as hard as you can.

6. Do not "telegraph" your punch. As in blocking, avoid the habit of "winding up" by drawing your fist back before you punch. You will give your punch away because it can be seen. Start your punch right from where your hands are in the ready position.

Figure 85

Figure 86

Sun Fist

You are in a horse stance, as in figure 87, and your fists are by your sides. Perform the sun punch as follows:

1. Bring your right fist to the centre of your body with the big knuckle of your right thumb against the hollow of your chest (under the breastbone). The front of your fist is facing upwards as in figure 88.

2. From that position, punch straight out towards the target. Your fist should end up in line with the centre of your body from where you have started. Make contact with the last three knuckles. See figure 89.

3. Notice that all the knuckles of your fist are vertical.

4. When you have completed the punch, withdraw your fist back to your side as in figure 90.

5. Then bring your left fist to the centre of your body with the big knuckle of your left thumb against the hollow of your chest. The front of your fist is facing upwards as in figure 91.

6. Punch towards the target in the same way as before with your left fist. See figure 92.

7. Withdraw your left fist back to your side.

8. Then repeat the above steps again with your right fist, etc.

The name "sun fist" comes from the vertical position of the fist after the punch is completed; it is like the Chinese character for "sun".

Figure 87

Figure 88

Figure 89

85

Figure 90

Figure 91

Figure 92

Corkscrew Punch

You are in a horse stance with your fists by your sides as in figure 93. Perform the corkscrew punch as follows:

1. Start with a right punch. Launch it directly from your side instead of placing your fist at the centre of your body first as in the sun punch.

2. Rotate your fist as it travels towards the target. Keep turning your punch until the back of your hand is facing upwards (instead of towards the side as in the sun punch). See figure 94.

3. The contact point of the corkscrew punch is with the first two knuckles of your fist (instead of the last three as in the sun fist). The corkscrew punch is a "sharp" punch while the sun fist is a "flatter" punch.

4. The punch should finish in line with the centre of your body.

5. When you have completed the punch, withdraw your fist back to your side.

6. Repeat the same movement with your left fist. (Your left fist starts moving towards the target at the same time that your right fist is withdrawing away from it. You left fist should be fully extended by the time your right fist is back at your side.) See figure 95.

7. Withdraw your left fist back to your side when you have completed the punch.

8. Then repeat the process over again with your right fist, etc.

Figure 93

Figure 94

Figure 95

Reverse Punch

To perform the reverse punch, start from a ready position with the left hand and foot forward as in figure 96. Then:

1. Pull your left "feeling hand" back to an emergency position close to the left side of your face with the palm facing towards you. At the same time, launch a right sun fist and lower your body by getting into a drop knee stance. See figure 97.

2. Your shoulders can finish square to your target as in figure 97 or...

3. ...the right shoulder could turn more towards the target as in figure 98. Your reach and the amount of power you deliver depend on how much you rotate.

4. The more you turn or "reverse" your shoulders, the more you would have to turn on the ball of your rear foot.

5. Tighten your fist at the end when the arm is fully extended.

6. Check to make sure that the punch finishes in line with the centre of your body. (If you turn your shoulders to the maximum, then your punch should be in line with your shoulders.)

7. Return to the ready position after you have completed the punch by pulling your right hand back into the emergency position and extending your left hand out.

8. Switch your stance and go through each movement with your other hand also.

Figure 96

Figure 97

Figure 98

90

Hammer Fist

You are in the ready position with the left hand and left foot forward as in figure 99. The hammer fist can be performed with either the "leading hand" or "reserve hand". Let's go through the steps on how to do it with the "reserve hand" first:

1. Raise the palm of your right "reserve hand" a little above your forehead with the palms facing out as in figure 100.

2. Then draw the back of your hand across your forehead and pull your elbow backwards as if though you are wiping the sweat off your forehead. Your palm is still pointing towards your target. See figure 101.

3. Begin to make a fist as you snap your elbow and upper arm forward. Tighten your fist at the moment of impact—not before. Make contact with the bottom of your fist. See figure 102.

4. Avoid swinging your arm out to the side when you deliver the strike. That will make the hammer fist less noticeable. It should travel straight towards the target.

5. Draw your left "leading hand" back into a "reserve hand" at the same time.

6. After you made contact with your target, get into a ready position again by extending your left "reserve hand" back out into a "leading hand". (You are in the same position that your were in before you started.)

7. Repeat steps 1 to 4 with your left "leading hand" also. In this case, you do not have to switch hands (like in step 6) to get back into the ready position.

8. Switch your front stance and go through each movement with your other hand also.

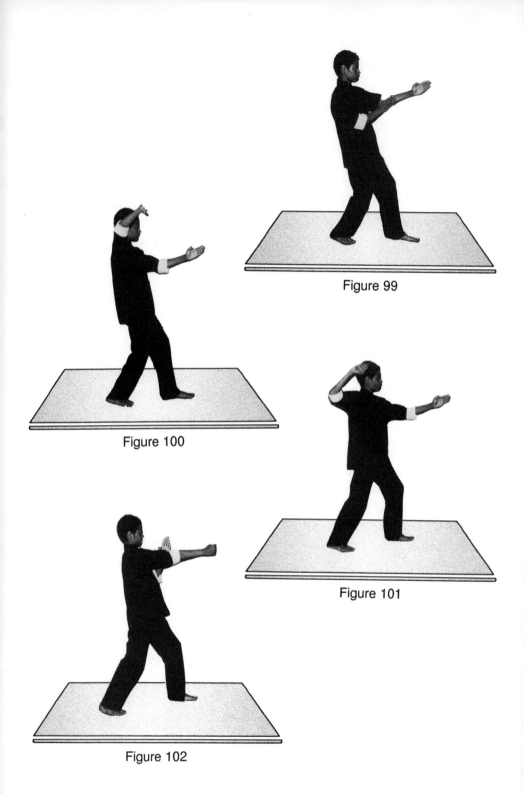

Figure 99

Figure 100

Figure 101

Figure 102

Back Fist

Start from a ready position with the left hand and left foot forward as in figure 103. You are going to throw the back fist with the "leading hand". Here are the steps in how it's done:

1. Raise the elbow of your left "leading hand" towards your target until your arm is parallel to the ground (with your thumb still pointing upwards) while you position your hand near your right shoulder at the same time. See figure 104.

2. Before the elbow gets pass the height of your shoulder, your arm should be fully extended (you should have completed step 3 and 4 below at this point).

3. Fully extend your hand towards your target when your elbow is in line with it. Do not draw your hand back before striking since your lower arm is already drawn back by the movement of your elbow as described in step (1).

4. Tighten your fist at the moment of impact—not before. A tightly clenched fist before delivery will tighten the arm as well, and all that tension will slow down your back fist. The arm should be relaxed enough to enable you to whip it towards the target.

5. The path your fist has taken is a straight line (even though you threw it at an angle). Notice the position of the arm in figure 105 after it reaches the target. It does not sway off to the side. It is almost as if though you had thrown a straight punch. Connection is made with the back of the fist.

6. Return to the ready position after you have made contact with your target.

7. Switch your stance and go through each movement with your other hand also.

Figure 103

Figure 104

Figure 105

94

Back Fist and Reverse Punch

After you become familiar with single punches, you can try various combinations. One popular combination is the back fist and reverse punch. Here are the steps involved:

1. Start from the ready position with the left hand and left foot forward as in figure 106.

2. Perform the back fist with your left "leading hand" as described in the last section. See figure 107 and 108.

3. Then bring the left hand back to the emergency position beside the left side of your face while you throw the reverse punch with your right hand as previously described. See figure 109. There is no pause between steps (2) and (3).

4. Return to the ready position after you have made contact with your target.

5. Switch your front stance and go through each movement with your other hand also.

Figure 106

Figure 107

Figure 108

Figure 109

Chapter 6

KICKING

Points to Remember:

In all the kicks that we will talk about, let's assume that you are in a ready position with your left "leading hand" and left foot forward. Here are some points to keep in mind:

1. Always consider the three things that we have mentioned earlier when you attempt any kick: safety, simplicity, and effectiveness.

2. Have an imaginary target in front of you when you are training by yourself.

3. At this level, we will mainly be using the rear leg for kicking because you will have more control.

4. From the ready position, notice that your "leading hand" is on the same side as your leading foot. So if your left foot is out, your left hand should be out.

5. When you kick with the rear leg, your "reserve hand" becomes your "feeling hand" by extending it out at the same time that the kick is thrown.

6. When you place you kicking leg back to the rear after the completion of the kick, your "leading hand" shifts back to a "reserve hand".

7. If you are kicking with the leading leg, you do not have to switch hands. In this case, your "feeling hand" during the kick is the same as your "feeling hand" before the kick.

8. Whether you are kicking with the leading leg or with the back leg, keep your "reserve hand" up during the kick; there is more of a tendency to drop this hand than the "feeling hand".

9. A lot of students forget to turn or pivot on the supporting leg. Some kicks, like the side kick and roundhouse kick, can create a lot of twist against the knee when the upper body is turning and your supporting leg does not turn with it. By pivoting, you will relieve a lot of this pressure and prevent injuries to your knees in the future.

10. The more you do your stretches, the easier it will be for you to perform your kicks.

11. To avoid pulling a muscle, warm up first before you practise your kicks.

12. Refrain from doing a lot of powerful kicks—especially snap kicks—without a striking bag or padded shield to cushion them. Kicking "thin air" can produce a lot of stress on your knees.

13. Do not favour one leg more than the other when you kick.

14. Do not get into the habit of using your legs more than your hands. Punching is just as important as kicking.

15. In a serious situation, do not get too fancy with your footwork. Unlike a tournament or any other friendly competition, you will not get a second chance if a certain technique does not work.

Front Kick

The front kick is the first of several kicks that you will learn. It is a good introductory kick to prepare you for more difficult ones. Perform the kick as follows:

1. Get into a ready position and face your target with your left hand and left foot forward as in figure 110. You are going to kick with the right rear leg.

2. Drag the right foot forward (on the ball of the foot) until it leaves the floor as in figure 111.

3. Continue thrusting your leg towards your target. At the end of the movement: flex the toes up towards you, point your foot forward, and thrust your leg out. The point of contact is with the balls of your foot. See figure 112.

4. You do not have to cock your lower leg back before you kick because it is already slightly bent. You just have to straighten it with full extension.

5. The instep could also be used as the contact point depending on the angle and height of the target. Flex your toes down away from you to expose that part of the foot just before you make contact. See figure 113.

6. The foot of the supporting leg should automatically turn at 45 degrees by pivoting on the ball of the foot. See figure 114.

7. Follow through by turning and pushing your hips forward and squaring up to your target to give you extra power and reach. To avoid losing your balance, do not lean back too much.

8. Extend your right hand out at the same time that you kick.

9. After you kick, immediately pull the kicking leg back to the rear and withdraw your right hand back into a "reserve hand". You are in the ready stance again.

10. Switch your ready position and stance and practise with your left leg also.

Figure 110

Figure 111

Figure 112

Figure 113

Figure 114

101

Roundhouse Kick

This kick is called the roundhouse because it starts off the same way as the front kick, but then it changes direction and goes sideways. Perform the kick as follows:

1. From the ready position with left hand and foot forward, as in figure 115, you are going to kick with the right rear leg.

2. Drag the right foot forward in a straight like (on the ball of the foot) until it leaves the floor. Continue that movement towards the target. See figure 116.

3. Then turn your supporting foot until its heel is almost facing the front as in figure 117. (The higher you intend to kick, the more you have to pivot.)

4. The hip of your kicking leg should turn at the same time until it is on top of your left hip; this will rotate your kicking leg until its knee is pointing to the side. See figure 117.

5. Again, it is not necessary to pull the lower leg back because it is already bent.

6. Once you get to this stage, immediately straighten out your leg and drive it (not just the lower leg) sideways towards the target. There is little sideways movement before you reach it.

7. At the same time, flex your toes outwards away from you to expose the instep as the striking part of your foot. See figure 118. (Avoid making contact with your toes or any part near your toes instead of your instep; that can be painful—especially if you are not wearing shoes.)

8. The movements of the hands are the same as in the previous kick.

9. Upon completion, immediately pull the kicking leg back to the rear and assume the ready stance again.

10. Go through the above steps with your left leg also by switching your ready position and stance.

Figure 115

Figure 116

Figure 117

Figure 118

Side Kick

The side kick starts off the same way as the front kick (in steps 1 and 2) and the roundhouse kick (in steps 1 to 3). Perform the the kick as follows:

1. From the ready position with your right hand and right foot forward, as in figure 119, you are going to kick with the left rear leg.

2. Drag the left foot forward in a straight line (on the ball of your foot) until it leaves the floor. Continue this movement towards the target. See figure 120.

3. The supporting foot should start turning as you kick until its heel is almost facing the target. (The higher you intend to kick, the more you have to pivot.)

4. The hip of your kicking leg should turn at the same time until your knee is pointing more towards the floor (instead of to the side as in the roundhouse kick). See figure 121.

5. Flex your toes inwards towards you (instead of away from you as in the roundhouse kick) to expose your heel. Your foot is about 45 degrees from the floor. See figure 122. The striking area is from the middle of the foot to the heel.

6. Again, you do not have to pull the lower leg back before you kick. It is already bent. You simply thrust it out towards the target with full extension.

7. The kick should be completed by the time you finish turning on your supporting leg.

8. The kicking leg and the abdomen are tense at the point of impact to transmit the force behind this powerful kick.

9. Again, the movements of the hands are the same as in the previous kicks.

10. After you kick, immediately pull the kicking leg back to the rear and assume the ready stance again.

11. Switch your ready position and stance and practise with your other leg also.

Figure 119

Figure 120

Figure 121

Figure 122

Back Kick

The back kick is almost identical to the side kick. Note the following differences when you attempt it:

1. Start from a ready position with your right hand and right foot forward as in figure 123. You are going to kick with your right leading leg (instead of with your rear leg as in the previous kicks).

2. Instead of dragging the rear foot forward, pivot on the heel of the rear foot and on the ball of the leading foot until both heels are in a straight line with the target. See figure 124.

3. Immediately drag your right foot towards you until you are in a side-cat stance as in figure 125.

4. Your right "leading hand" is still out, and your left "reserve hand" is held close to your face.

5. From here, flex your toes (in the same direction as in the side kick) and thrust your right leg towards your target. The contact point is the lower part of your foot around your heel. Your leg should be fully extended. The toes of your kicking leg should be facing down towards the floor (as oppose to 45 degrees in the side kick). See figure 126.

6. Upon completion of the kick, bring the foot back to the side cat stance and then turn back into the ready position.

7. Switch your front stance and go through the movement with your other leg also.

Figure 123

Figure 124

Figure 125

Figure 126

109

Double Roundhouse Kick

The double roundhouse kick is made up of two roundhouse kicks. It is a good deceptive kick if your timing is correct. Perform the kick as follows:

1. You are in a ready position with your left hand and left foot forward. You are going to kick with the right rear leg. See figure 127.

2. Throw the first kick as you would normally throw a roundhouse kick except keep it low—about knee high. See figure 128. Then pull your kicking leg back with the knee still pointing to the side.

3. Without placing the kicking foot back on the ground, raise it higher and release another roundhouse. Deliver the second kick with more force. See figure 129.

4. You do not have to turn that much on the supporting foot for the first kick because it is low. To get the height behind the second kick, you have to pivot more. If the second kick is as high as your head, then the heel of your supporting foot would almost be in a straight line with your target. How much you pivot depends on the height of your kick and your flexibility.

5. You should have the intention of hitting your target with the first kick even though you are just using it to set up your second kick; so in that sense, it is not actually a fake. Once your opponent drops his or her guard, you kick high.

6. Remember to keep the hands out during the kick.

7. After you completed the second kick, immediately pull the kicking leg back to the rear and assume the ready stance.

8. Practise with your left leg also.

Figure 127

Figure 128

Figure 129

111

Spinning Back Kick

The spinning back kick is a combination of a spin plus a back kick. Here's how it's done:

1. Get into a ready position with your left hand and left foot forward. The kick will be done with your right rear leg. See figure 130.

2. Start by spinning clockwise (either on both heels or the balls of your feet at the same time) away from your target. Keep turning until you are able to see your target again over your right shoulder. See figure 131.

3. Pull your left "leading hand" back to the emergency position close to your face and extend your right "reserve hand" out at the end of the turn.

4. The thumb of your right "leading hand" is facing down since it is more comfortable and natural to rotate the right arm along with your body.

5. From that position, drag your right foot along a straight line towards your target. Then flex your toes and thrust your leg out in the same manner as the back kick. See figure 132.

6. The spin is not abrupt or violent. It is fast, but it should not be so fast that you sacrifice your balance.

7. To improve your balance, turn and see your target first before you kick. As you progress, you will almost see the target and kick at the same time.

8. Switch your stance and try this kick with the left leg also. In this case, you will be turning in the other direction.

Figure 130

Figure 131

Figure 132

113

Chapter 7

FOOTWORK

Points to Remember:

Footwork is an important part of self-defence because:

1. It allows you to get close to your target.

2. It will also help you to get out of the way of an oncoming punch or kick.

At this level, we will only concentrate on how to close some of the gap between you and your target. The two types of movement that we are going to cover are the "cross-over side kick" and the "hopping side kick".

We are only using a side kick as an example. Once you become familiar with that kick, the following techniques will come more natural: cross-over roundhouse kick, cross-over back fist, hopping roundhouse kick, and hopping front kick.

We will cover those types punches and kicks, along with how to use your footwork to avoid getting hit, in the next manual.

Cross-Over Side Kick

The footwork involved in the cross-over sidekick allows you to get closer to your target. Here are the steps involved:

1. Face your target in a ready position with your left hand and left foot forward as in figure 133.

2. Start by stepping in (about one foot) with your left foot.

3. Then slide your rear foot (your right foot) in front of your left foot as in figure 134.

4. From that position, kick with your left leg. Follow the same procedures as given in the section on the "Side Kick". See figure 135.

5. The movement of your hands are the same as in the side kick.

6. After you kick, immediately place the kicking leg back down in front of you and assume the ready stance again.

7. Practise this kick with your right leg also.

Figure 133

Figure 134

Figure 135

116

Hopping Side Kick

The hopping side kick is another kick that is used to get closer to your target when it is not within reach. Let's go over the stages of this kick:

1. Get into a ready position and face your target with your left hand and left foot forward as in figure 136. You are going to kick with your rear leg.

2. Drag the right foot forward in a straight line (on the ball of your foot) until it leaves the floor. Continue this movement towards the target. See figure 137.

3. Now instead of just pivoting on your balancing foot at a fixed spot as you normally would in a regular side kick, skip in and pivot at the same time. Remember, you are not jumping, you are hopping. Stay as close to the floor as possible while you hop and pivot at the same time. The heel of your supporting leg should end up facing towards your target. See figure 138.

4. The distance from where you started on your supporting leg (see arrow on figure 137) to where you ended up on your supporting leg (see arrow on figure 138) is how far you have advanced. Do not try to cover a lot of distance. Keep your hop short for balance and control.

5. When the hip of your kicking leg is turned up, thrust the side kick out as previously described. See figure 138.

6. The movement of your hands are the same as in the side kick.

7. After you kick, immediately pull the kicking leg back and assume the ready stance again. Practise this kick with your other leg also.

Figure 136

Figure 137

Figure 138

118

Chapter 8

APPLICATIONS

Points to Remember:

In this chapter, you are going to apply what you have learned so far. We are assuming that you have tried your best to avoid any direct confrontation and that you have no choice but to defend yourself.

Our applications fall into two categories: Blocking and Counter Attack. Counter attack means that you are going to deal with an attack that is directed against you (in this case, by blocking) and launch an attack of your own. Go over again the "Points to Remember" in the chapter on "Blocking".

Whether you block or counter attack someone's attack, keep these additional points in mind:

1. Do not plan your block. For example, do not say to yourself, "OK, I think he is going to throw a side kick. I am going to block it with an Outside Block."

2. Do not plan your counter attack. For example, do not say to yourself, "OK, I think he is going to throw a front kick, I am going to block it with a Low Block, and then I am going to step in an throw a Reverse Punch."

3. When we tell you not to plan your blocks and counter attacks, we are not saying that you must stop thinking altogether.

What we actually mean is that we do not want you to think in a certain way: we do not want you to guess. Guessing will only slow down your reaction.

4. Do not wait for a block by constantly looking at the other person's hands or feet before a punch or kick is thrown.

5. All blocks and counter attacks should be performed instinctively or automatically.

6. At this level, you are only going to counter attack with the reverse punch. We want you to get used to the idea that a punch is you main weapon because it is faster than a kick.

7. When you train on your own, always have an imaginary target in front of you (even when you are just blocking). Otherwise, you will misjudge your distance, and your strikes will fall short of your target in a real situation.

8. Practise the following blocks and counter attacks until they become second nature (until you can perform them without guessing).

Blocking

An attack can come above your guard, at the same level as your guard, or below your guard. In this section, you will deal with each of those situations by blocking:

Hammer Fist/High Block

The high block is used against attacks coming above your guard (either directly overhead or a bit off to the side). In this case, a hammer fist is thrown by a taller opponent. Here's how to meet it with a high block:

1. You and your partner are facing each other in a left front stance as in figure 139.

2. Your partner is about to throws a hammer fist directly over your head as in figure 140.

3. Raise you "leading hand" into a high block as in figure 141.

4. Flex your wrist back at the same time to tighten your forearm muscles.

5. Do not hold your blocking arm directly over your head and wait for the hammer fist to reach you. Block into it before the hammer fist descends down too far. It is almost like a jamming motion.

6. Make sure that the point of contact is below the wrist. You need more support since the strike is coming directly overhead. The slope of your arm will deflect the force of the hammer fist.

7. Immediately return to the ready position after you have completed the block.

8. You can also use your "reserve hand" if the strike is coming at you from an angle that is hard to reach with your other hand. In this case, pull your "leading hand" back to an emergency position while you are blocking into the hammer fist with your "reserve hand". Switch your hands again and return to the ready position after you have completed the block.

9. Change into a right front stance and practise each movement with your other hand also.

Figure 139

Figure 140

Figure 141

122

Back Fist/Thrust Block

A back fist is hard to block because sometimes it goes around your guard. A thrust block is a good reply. Here are the steps involved:

1. You and your partner are facing each other in a left front stance as in figure 142.

2. Your partner intends to throw a left back fist at you as in figure 143.

3. Meet the oncoming strike by blocking into it (instead of waiting for it) with a left thrust block. See figure 144.

4. Launch the block in a forward jamming motion instead of swinging it out to the side.

5. Immediately return to the ready position after you have completed the block.

6. You can also use your "reserve hand" if your partner suddenly delivers a back fist with his other hand. In this case, the back fist will be coming from the other direction. As you thrust your "reserve hand" forward, pull your "leading hand" back into the emergency position at the same time. Return to your ready position again as in step (1) after you have completed the block. It is a good drill to mix it up by throwing in a right back fist now and then. Do it slowly at first; then pick up speed as your reaction improves.

7. Change into a right front stance and repeat each movement with your other hand also.

Figure 142

Figure 143

Figure 144

124

Back Fist/Palm Block

Another answer to a back fist is a palm block. The palm block has more reach, and it is a good block to use if you detect the back fist early. As we mentioned before, you can use your "leading hand" or your "reserve hand". The following is an example of applying your "reserve hand":

1. You and your partner are facing each other in a left front stance as in figure 145.

2. Your partner intends to throw a left back fist at you as in figure 146.

3. Meet the oncoming strike by blocking into it in a forward and sideways motion with your right palm while pulling your left "leading hand" back into the emergency position at the same time.

4. Avoid committing your block too much towards the side.

5. If it is done early enough, the blocking arm is about 45 degrees from your body. See figure 147.

6. Immediately return to the ready position as in step (1) after you have completed the block.

7. You can also use your "leading hand" if your partner suddenly delivers a back fist with his other hand. In this case the back fist will be coming from the other direction. Return to the ready position after you have completed the block. Again, it is a good drill to mix it up by throwing in a right back fist now and then. Do it slowly at first; then pick up speed as your reaction improves.

8. Change into a right front stance and repeat each movement with your other hand also.

Figure 145

Figure 146

Figure 147

126

Front Kick/Low Block

A front kick is coming straight towards you, and it is about to go under your guard. A good reply would be a low block as follows:

1. You and your partner are facing each other in a left front stance as in figure 148.

2. Your partner delivers a front kick, and its target is below the level of your leading hand.

3. Meet the oncoming kick by blocking into it with a low block. If it is done early enough, the blocking arm is about 45 degrees from your body. Try to take the steam out of the kick before it picks up speed or before it gets too close to you. See figure 149.

4. Switch your stance and go through each movement with your other hand also.

Figure 148

127

Figure 149

Counter Attack

Instead of just blocking, you are now going to counter by blocking and delivering an attack of your own. The thrust block and reverse punch and the low block and reverse punch will be covered in this section.

Thrust Block and Reverse Punch

Read over again the information that we have given about the thrust block in this chapter and in the chapter on "Blocking". The following is how you would put it together with a reverse punch to counter against a punch or kick:

1. From the ready position with the left hand and left foot forward, block the oncoming punch or kick with a thrust block by extending your "leading hand" forward along the centre of your body. See figure 150.

2. Once you have made contact, withdraw the blocking hand to the side of your left ear while you deliver a reverse punch with your right "reserve hand" as in figure 151. Figure 152 shows another view.

3. Go over each movement in a right front stance also.

Figure 150

Figure 151

Figure 152

129

Low Block and Reverse Punch

Read over again the information that we have given about the low block in this chapter and in the chapter on "Blocking". The following is how you would put it together with a reverse punch to counter against a kick that goes below your guard:

1. From the ready position with the left hand and left foot forward, use your left "leading hand" to block the oncoming kick with a low block. See figure 153.

2. The moment you completed your block, withdraw the blocking hand back to an emergency position beside the side of your ear while you deliver a reverse punch with your right "reserve hand". See figure 154.

3. Figure 155 shows another view.

4. Switch your stance and go through each movement with your other hand also.

Figure 153

Figure 154

Figure 155

131

Chapter 9

STRANGULATION

Points to Remember:

What if someone grabs you before you can punch, kick, or counter his or her attack? As we have said earlier, he or she may be so close that there is no room for you to use your favourite kick or punch. After you have been seized by someone who is a lot stronger than you and who intends to do the most harm in the shortest period of time, it is common for your attacker to follow up with a strangle hold.

You have tried your best to avoid such a situation; but, for some reason, your were not as sharp as you should be. Maybe you were tired, deep in thought, or feeling depressed about something. Whatever the reason, you are taken by surprise. So, what do you do?

The important thing to keep in mind is not to panic. If you panic, there will be indecision. Indecision means hesitation, and hesitation is time wasted. Do not waste any time when you are up against a strangler.

To avoid indecision, we want you to become familiar with the three techniques in this chapter inside out until they become a reflex action. If we give you more than that at this stage, you will only forget them. You might have a terrific memory and be able to remember dozens of techniques when you practise on your own or with someone else; but when a real situation occurs, your mind will tend to go blank. That is the last thing you want to happen.

You have to react fast because his or her hands are around your throat. You are deprived of oxygen, and you will past out within seconds. Moreover, your throat is a sensitive area; it is easy to damage or bruise vital parts there which in turn will affect your breathing.

To break a throat hold, you have two options:

1. You can inflict pain (by hitting him or her) and break the hold at the same time and then run. Always try this option first because it is more effective.

2. You can break the hold first and then hit and/or run.

"Why do you have to break the grip first?" you might ask.

There are two common situations that require you to break the hold before you can do anything else:

1. When you cannot reach your target.

2. When your strike did not cause enough pain for your attacker to let go of you completely.

In the following pages, the "Spear Hand' technique is an example of inflicting pain and breaking the hold at the same time. "Dropping the Bridge" and "Buddha Clasp Hands" techniques are examples of breaking the hold first.

Spear Hand

The first release against a throat hold is the "Spear Hand". It is a quick and effective technique which can also work if you are sitting or lying down. This strike will give you more reach than a punch, and that will be to your advantage if your attacker has long arms.

Please keep in mind that serious injury can result when you actually perform the following steps:

1. Your opponent has a front throat hold on you as in figure 156.

2. Extend all of your fingers and close them until they look like the head of a spear. Place the "spear hand" on the throat below the larynx as in figure 157.

3. Then thrust it forward in a quick and sharp jab as in figure 158.

4. You place your striking hand on the target first at medium speed instead of trying to hit it at full speed for two reasons: first, you want to make sure that you hit the target; and second, the change of speed is deceiving. (It is like throwing a "change up" when he is expecting a "fast ball".)

Even a minimal amount of force is enough to break the hold and inflict serious injury. It is very effective against a stronger attacker.

Do not try this move on anyone even if he or she knows what to expect. Serious damage can result if excessive force is used. We suggest that you practise on an imaginary target to avoid any accident.

Figure 156

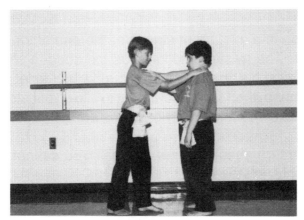

Figure 157

Figure 158

135

Dropping the Bridge

The second type of release from a throat hold is called "Dropping the Bridge". Learn how to break the grip first in steps 1 to 4 before following through with steps 5 and 6.

1. Cross both your arms over your partner's arms to trap them. See figure 159.

2. As you start turning as in figure 160, put the weight of your body behind the turn by stepping towards the rear and a bit to the side with your left foot at the same time.

3. Drop into a left front stance at the end of the turn as in figure 161. The twisting motion plus the sudden shift of your weight against his arms will force your partner to let go. (If you are left handed, then turn to your right to allow your stronger arm to come into contact with your partner's arm.)

4. The turn should not be gradual. You cannot break his grip by applying steady pressure.

5. After the grip is broken, you are in a good position to throw a back kick or a side kick. (Do not throw a roundhouse because it is not as powerful as a back or side kick.)

6. After you have thrown the kick, you will be facing the direction where you will be running. Replace the kicking leg on the ground ahead of you and push off with your other foot and RUN.

Steps 5 and 6 can also be used as an effective counter attack if your attacker had grabbed you again after you had broken his or her grip.

Figure 159

Figure 160

Figure 161

137

Buddha Clasp Hands

The third type of release from a front strangulation is call the Buddha Clasp Hand. Break the hold as follows:

1. Clasp the palms of your hands together with your fingers pointing upwards and aim them between your partner's arms as in figure 162.

2. Then drive them upwards to pry the arms apart. The power comes from the wedging force of your arms. Joining them together gives you more power and prevents either of them from collapsing. Get into the habit of thrusting your arms straight up. You will not get the full force behind your thrust if it veers off to one side.

3. Once the hold is weakened or broken, separate your hands as in figure 163 and push them forward against your partner's lower arms with full extension as in figure 164. Your partner's arms will spread farther apart. If your timing is right, you can also upset his or her balance. (Do not separate your hands before your wedged arms come into contact with his or her lower arms.)

4. There should be no pause between the upward thrust, the forward spreading of the hands, and the push. You do not want him or her to recover his or her grip.

5. When the arms are separated, your partner is wide open to a front kick or reverse punch.

6. After that, do not forget to RUN.

Figure 162

Figure 163

Figure 164

139

Chapter 10

TESTING

Why Tests?

Once you are confident that you know everything up to this point, you should not have any problems with your test. If you are in any of our classes, you will be told ahead of time when and where it will be held. If you are already taking lessons elsewhere, what we have to say in this chapter will also help you.

"Why bother with tests at all?" you might ask.

That is a good question. Different instructors have their own reasons for giving them. Let us tell you why we give them.

For one thing, they tells us how much you know and how well you display what you know.

Another reason is that we want to see how well you conduct yourself in a test. You might feel nervous, you might have trouble thinking clearly, you might have trouble keeping your confidence, you might worry about making mistakes, you might feel awkward... It is common to have some of those same feelings when you confront an unexpected situation on the "street", and we want you to learn how to deal with them.

An effective way to overcome nervousness and lack of confidence is by knowing your material well. If you do not know it well, then that is good enough a reason to be nervous. Of course, it is possible that you can be nervous and know your material well, but you will not be "that" nervous. It is OK to be a little nervous. That is perfectly normal. In fact, it is good to be a little nervous. When your adrenaline is flowing, it helps you to think clearly; your senses become sharp, and you become more alert.

After you have taken a lot of tests, you will get to a point where you will not feel nervous at all. That is the type of control we really want you to have as part of your Self-Defence.

AFTERWORD

We hope that you have enjoyed reading this book and have learned something from it.

If you want to write to us for any reason (e.g., about any problem that you might have, about our upcoming courses and seminars, about information concerning our schools, etc.), we will be glad to hear from you.

Write to:

Hugh Wilson & John Yee
c/o Outgoing Press,
P.O. Box 45507,
Don Mills, Ontario
M3C 3S4

ORDER FORM

To order extra copies of this book, please inquire at the bookstore where it was purchased. Otherwise, fill in this form and mail it along with your cheque or money order for $19.95 plus $3.00 shipping (shipping is free for orders totaling three or more books). Make payment to Outgoing Press. Please clearly print your name, address, and postal (zip) code.

Please send me _____ copies of
Not Just Another Self-Defence Book
1st Edition, ISBN 1-896212-01-8

Payment with order: _____ @ $19.95 each plus $3.00 shipping. (Shipping is free for orders totalling 3 books or more.)

I am paying by: ❑ Cheque   ❑ Money Order

Name: _____
Address: _____
City: _____
Province / State: _____
Postal / Zip Code: _____

Send all orders to:

Outgoing Press
P.O. Box 45507, 747 Don Mills Road
Don Mills, Ontario, Canada
M3C 3S4

ORDER FORM

To order extra copies of this book, please inquire at the bookstore where it was purchased. Otherwise, fill in this form and mail it along with your cheque or money order for $19.95 plus $3.00 shipping (shipping is free for orders totaling three or more books). Make payment to Outgoing Press. Please clearly print your name, address, and postal (zip) code.

Please send me _____ copies of
Not Just Another Self-Defence Book
1st Edition, ISBN 1-896212-01-8

Payment with order: _____ @ $19.95 each plus $3.00 shipping. (Shipping is free for orders totalling 3 books or more.)

I am paying by: ❑ Cheque   ❑ Money Order

Name: _____
Address: _____
City: _____
Province / State: _____
Postal / Zip Code: _____

Send all orders to:

Outgoing Press
P.O. Box 45507, 747 Don Mills Road
Don Mills, Ontario, Canada
M3C 3S4